THE

MOUNTAINS
OF
QUILT

VOYAGER BOOKS
HARCOURT BRACE & COMPANY
San Diego   New York   London

THE

MOUNTAINS

OF

QUILT

Story by NANCY WILLARD

Pictures by TOMIE dePAOLA

To all the people who ride Amtrak, especially those who take the
Lake Shore Limited to Cleveland,

Elyria,

Sandusky,

and Detroit

—N. W.

To Peter,

Robin,

Nick,

and Will

—T. deP.

First Voyager Books edition 1997
Voyager Books is a registered trademark of
Harcourt Brace & Company.

Library of Congress Cataloging-in-Publication Data
Willard, Nancy.
   The mountains of quilt.
   Summary: Four magicians lose their magic carpet which
eventually finds its way into the center of a grandmother's quilt.
   [1. Magicians — Fiction.   2. Grandmothers — Fiction.
3. Quilting — Fiction.]   I. dePaola, Tomie, ill.   II. Title.
PZ7.W6553Mo   1987   [E]   86-19577
ISBN 0-15-256010-6
ISBN 0-15-201480-2 (pbk.)

F E D C B A

Printed in Singapore

In the Mountains of Cleveland there lived a magician. And in the valley below the magician's kitchen window lived my grandmother. The magician did not know about my grandmother—he seldom looked out of the kitchen window—and my grandmother did not know about the magician. She had never seen the Mountains of Cleveland. The magician had made the mountains, and nobody could see them but himself and three magician friends with mountains of their own, and the magpie, who saw everything.

The magpie flew between the Magician of the Mountains of Cleveland and my grandmother and kept an eye on both of them. Both of them lived alone.

My grandmother often praised the thoughtfulness of the magpie, who visited her on Monday, Wednesday, and Friday. On fine mornings she sat in the backyard and made crazy quilts. Oh, such quilts! My grandmother had a big bag of scraps, for she never threw anything away, and she never minded when the magpie snitched a few, because he always brought nice presents in return. A gold button, a silver key, a Canadian penny.

Once upon a time, on a Tuesday, the magpie flew over my grandmother's clothesline, where she had just hung a magnificent quilt: red as embers, green as ferns, with a border of silver and gold stars on sky-blue velvet. In the middle of the quilt was a gaping hole. My grandmother was standing with her hands on her hips and muttering to herself:

"At my age what I really need is a nice scrap for the center."

Now it happened that on Tuesdays the magician had lunch with his three friends, the Magician of the Mountains of Sandusky, the Magician of the Mountains of Elyria, and the Magician of the Mountains of Detroit. They took turns meeting at each other's houses.

Every fourth Tuesday they met at the house of the Magician of the Mountains of Cleveland, who had a spell for making chocolate pudding with cream, and leftovers. The leftovers he put out for the magpie. The spell was old and in need of repair. Once it brought a peacock instead of a pudding. Sometimes it forgot the cream. Today it forgot the leftovers.

After lunch the magicians entertained each other with magic.

The Magician of the Mountains of Elyria had invented a pair of spectacles for seeing the remarkable animals that lived on their mountains. The four magicians took turns putting on the spectacles and admiring the lavender crows.

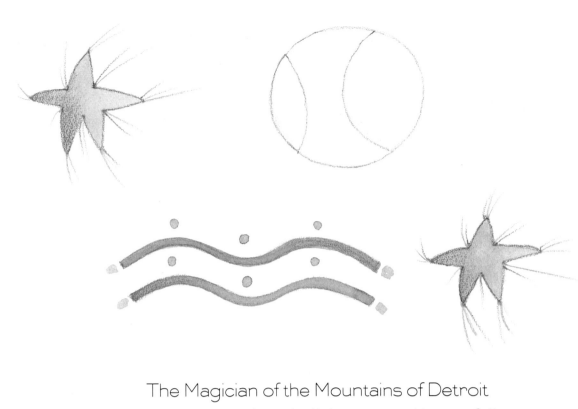

The Magician of the Mountains of Detroit
had invented a baseball that turned into a full
moon when the sun went down. Very useful,
he pointed out, for spells requiring moonlight
on nights when the moon turns off her lamp.
He tossed it up and it stayed there.

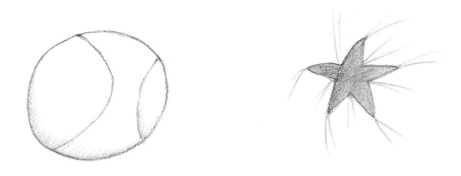

By the light of the baseball moon the Magician of the Mountains of Sandusky said he had invented a pair of musical sneakers. When you untied the laces, the sneakers sang as if with a thousand voices. Unfortunately he had forgotten to bring them.

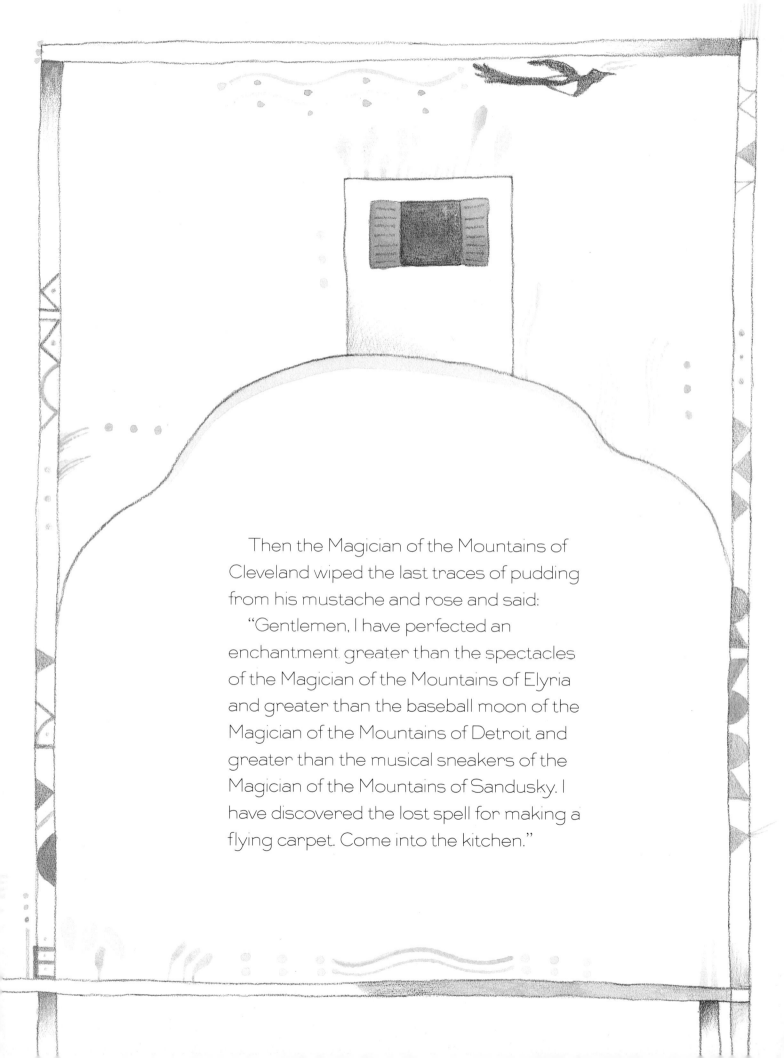

Then the Magician of the Mountains of Cleveland wiped the last traces of pudding from his mustache and rose and said:

"Gentlemen, I have perfected an enchantment greater than the spectacles of the Magician of the Mountains of Elyria and greater than the baseball moon of the Magician of the Mountains of Detroit and greater than the musical sneakers of the Magician of the Mountains of Sandusky. I have discovered the lost spell for making a flying carpet. Come into the kitchen."

The kitchen was full of dirty dishes. Perched on the kitchen windowsill, the magpie cocked his head and peered this way, that way, every which way for leftovers.

In trooped the magicians. From the oven the Magician of the Mountains of Cleveland took a covered dish, and from the covered dish he drew a cloth the size of a man's handkerchief.

"What a lovely shade of red!" exclaimed the Magician of the Mountains of Elyria.

"You mean blue," said the Magician of the Mountains of Detroit.

"I thought it was green," said the Magician of the Mountains of Sandusky.

"I was mistaken," said the Magician of the Mountains of Elyria. "It's cloth of gold."

"You mean cloth of silver," said the Magician of the Mountains of Detroit.

The Magician of the Mountains of Cleveland grinned.

"Gentlemen, it's magic," he said. "It's a magic carpet."

He blew on the carpet ever so lightly, and it darted to and fro over the heads of the magicians.

"It's nice," said the Magician of the Mountains of Detroit.

"It's nice but awfully small," said the Magician of the Mountains of Sandusky.

The Magician of the Mountains of Cleveland explained that to make a full-sized carpet would cost a great deal, as the materials were rare and expensive. But a small carpet had many uses. It could set the table and clear the dishes. It could bring you a cup of tea in the morning, if you got up and made the tea first. Of course there were problems. The carpet loved to speed around the house. Sometimes forks fell and plates flew and tea sloshed over the sofa and chairs.

"It's still a very young carpet," said the Magician of the Mountains of Cleveland. "In a few years it will settle down. Of course I never let it out of the house."

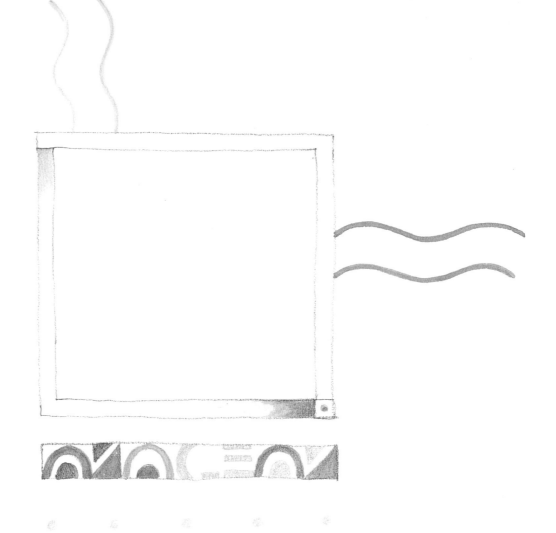

One minute the carpet was hovering by the open
window and the next minute the carpet was gone.
   "A genie has snatched your carpet!" cried the
Magician of the Mountains of Sandusky.

"A black cloud whirled it away!" cried the Magician of the Mountains of Detroit.

"No, the magpie stole it," said the Magician of the Mountains of Elyria. "The same magpie who visits me every Wednesday and every third Tuesday. I always give him my leftovers."

The Magician of the Mountains of Cleveland paled.

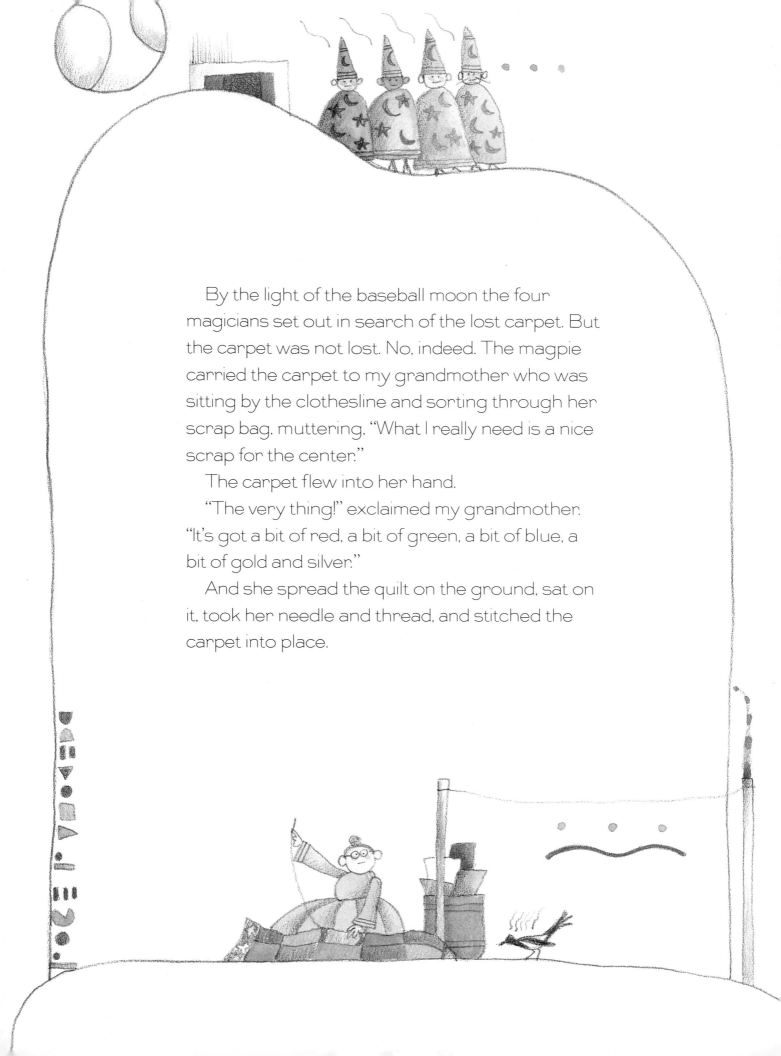

By the light of the baseball moon the four magicians set out in search of the lost carpet. But the carpet was not lost. No, indeed. The magpie carried the carpet to my grandmother who was sitting by the clothesline and sorting through her scrap bag, muttering, "What I really need is a nice scrap for the center."

The carpet flew into her hand.

"The very thing!" exclaimed my grandmother. "It's got a bit of red, a bit of green, a bit of blue, a bit of gold and silver."

And she spread the quilt on the ground, sat on it, took her needle and thread, and stitched the carpet into place.

She had no sooner pulled the last stitch than
the quilt rose into the air. My grandmother held
on hard—what else could she do? The carpet
was chasing the magpie. The magpie flew east,
the magpie flew straight to the house of the
Magician of the Mountains of Elyria, who had left
his kitchen window open. On the table stood a
freshly conjured pie. The quilt swooped into the
pantry, and the magpie tapped the pie with one
claw. Zip! It sprang to the quilt and made itself at
home.

But my grandmother saw no pie. She saw
nothing but the clouds around her.

"They look good enough to eat," she said to
herself.

The magpie flew west, the magpie flew straight to the house of the Magician of the Mountains of Detroit, who had left his dining room window open. On the table were five plates, conjured so clean that they sparkled. The quilt swooped into the dining room, and the magpie tapped the plates with his claw. Zap! The five plates rolled aboard my grandmother's quilt.

But my grandmother saw no plates. She saw nothing but the sky around her.

"Clean and sparkling," she said to herself. "It must have rained."

The magpie flew east, the magpie flew west, the magpie flew straight to the house of the Magician of the Mountains of Sandusky. The sneakers were snoozing on the front steps, singing to themselves, when the magpie tapped them with his claw, right shoe, left shoe. Thump! The sneakers walked right over to my grandmother's quilt and hopped aboard.

But my grandmother saw no shoes and heard no singing. She heard nothing but the wind tiptoeing around her.

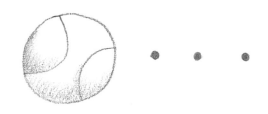

Under the baseball moon, the magicians scanned the sky. Suddenly the Magician of the Mountains of Detroit said:

"The sky is sending down an island."

The quilt sank lower.

"I see a powerful magician on a flying carpet," cried the Magician of the Mountains of Cleveland, "fifty times larger than mine."

"It's carrying my sneakers!" said the Magician of the Mountains of Sandusky.

"And my plates!" cried the Magician of the Mountains of Detroit.

"And my pie!" cried the Magician of the Mountains of Elyria.

It was at that moment my grandmother lost her spectacles. Without them, she was very nearsighted. She never saw the magpie tuck her spectacles into the right coat pocket of the Magician of the Mountains of Elyria. Nobody, not even the Magician of the Mountains of Elyria, saw the magpie take the magic spectacles from his left coat pocket and slip them into my grandmother's hand.

"Thank heaven!" said my grandmother and pushed the spectacles on her nose.

By the light of the baseball moon, the magicians looked at my grandmother and my grandmother looked at the magicians.

"Who are you? And where am I?" asked my grandmother.

"O most mighty enchantress," said the Magician of the Mountains of Elyria. "We are four magicians, tired and hungry, looking for a lost carpet."

"O most wonderful wizardess," said the Magician of the Mountains of Cleveland, "the center of your magic quilt looks very like my magic carpet."

"Does it?" said my grandmother. "Then sit right down and make yourselves at home."

She cut the pie—it was chock-full of blueberries—and passed it round, and the musical sneakers sang "Billy Boy" till the Magician of the Mountains of Sandusky put them on. When they had finished the pie, the four magicians and my grandmother bent forward to examine the patch of cloth at the center of her quilt.

But what was this? My grandmother's stitches were gone. All the pieces had grown together around the magician's carpet, which gleamed like a pond in a garden. Under the blue and green threads glimmered silver and gold fish.

"How could it be your carpet?" said my grandmother. "The magpie gave it to me."

"The magpie stole it," said the Magician of the Mountains of Cleveland.

He took out a tiny pair of scissors and tried to cut the carpet free, but he might have been cutting water for all the difference he made.

"Listen," said my grandmother, "I'm sorry about your carpet. Anytime you want to borrow my quilt, just let me know."

"Quilt?" exclaimed the Magician of the Mountains of Sandusky. "It's not a quilt. It's meadows and mountains running farther than the eye can see."

My grandmother shaded her eyes. She looked east, she looked west, she looked north, she looked south. On every side unrolled a country of marvelous beauty: ferns, waterfalls, and green fields tufted with poppies as red as embers, where the golden cows and silver sheep grazed and gamboled together.

But what astonished her most was her own house and her clothesline and her big bag of scraps right there in the middle of the greenest field.

"O mighty Magician of the Mountains of Quilt, we would be honored if you would join us for lunch on Tuesdays," said the Magician of the Mountains of Detroit.

"I'll think about it," said my grandmother.

She's still thinking about it—when is there time for lunch on Tuesday? The cows have to be milked, the sheep have to be sheared, the garden weeded. And the magicians haven't called. She thinks maybe they've moved. The magpie comes every day.

When I visit my grandmother, I see nothing but the clean blue sky and the clouds and the quilt airing on the clothesline. But when she throws the quilt over me at night, she tells me about the Mountains of Quilt, and how every night she weeds and milks and shears and sits by the waterfall and sews.

"Can I go there?"

"Not without the magic spectacles."

"Can I wear the magic spectacles?"

"Didn't need 'em," she says, "so I gave them to the magpie. My old ones are better for reading."

"Tomorrow is Friday. Can I see the magpie?"

"Didn't you see him today? He brought me a button. Tuesday he brought me a key. Wednesday he brought me a Canadian penny. I wonder what he'll bring me on Friday?"

The original drawings in this book were done in colored pencil and Rohtring
    watercolor on Rives 100% rag bristol.
The original manuscript was typed on a 1936 L. C. Smith and Corona
    manual typewriter.
The text type was set in Burin Sans by Central Graphics, San Diego,
    California.
The hand-lettered display type was based on Harry Thin and set by
    Thompson Type, San Diego, California.
Printed and bound by Tien Wah Press, Singapore
This book was printed on Leykam recycled paper, which contains more
    than 20 percent postconsumer waste and has a total recycled content of
    at least 50 percent.
Designed by Dalia Hartman
Production supervision by Warren Wallerstein and Ginger Boyer